THARSIS CITY

THE WONDER OF MARS

BY A.L. COLLINS

ILLUSTRATED BY TOMISLAV TIKULIN

raintree

a Capstone company — publishers for children

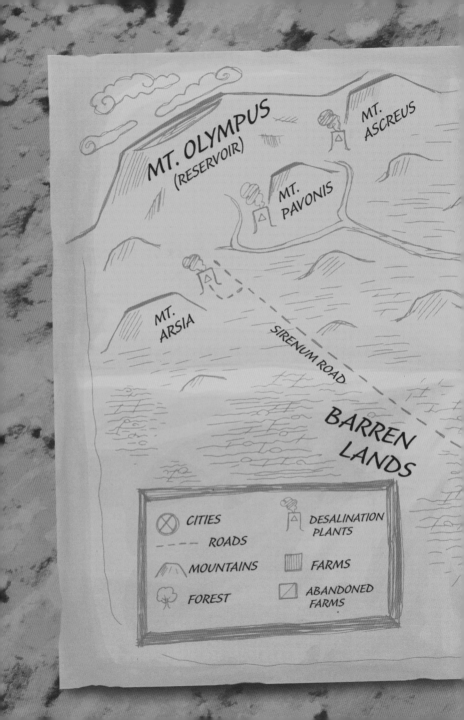

Belle Song

Thirteen-year-old Belle can be headstrong and stubborn. Her curiosity and sense of adventure often get her into trouble. Still, she has a good heart and is passionate about fairness. She is fiercely loyal to her friends.

Yun and Zara Song

Belle's parents sometimes seem really strict. But Yun has a great sense of humour, which Belle both loves and is embarrassed by. Zara has a generous heart, which has taught Belle not to judge others too quickly.

Melody

Melody is an old model 3X Personal Home Helper android. She was given to Belle by her grandmother before she passed away. Melody is Belle's best friend and protector, and enjoys telling bad jokes to seem more human.

MAIN INHABITANTS

Lucas Walker

Lucas is Belle's neighbour and classmate. He is part Sulux and part human. Meeting new people is not easy for him. But once he knows someone, his adventurous side emerges. He is full of ideas, which sometimes gets him and his friends into trouble.

Ta'al

Ta'al and her family are Nabian, an ancient alien race from another star system. Born and raised on Mars, Ta'al is intelligent and curious. She enjoys exploring and adventure, and quickly becomes Belle's closest friend on Mars.

Raider

Raider is a hybrid wolf-dog. These animals were bred to be tame pets, but some of them became wild. After Raider is rescued by Belle, he becomes a faithful and protective companion.

It is the year 2335. Life on Earth is very difficult. Widespread disease, a lack of resources and a long war against intelligent robots has caused much suffering. Some Terrans, those who are from Earth, have moved to the Lunar Colony in search of a better life. But the Moon is overcrowded and has limited resources. Other families have chosen to move to Mars instead. With the help of two alien races – the Sulux and the Nabians – the red planet was transformed to support life nearly 200 years ago.

Hoping to find a better life, Yun and Zara Song and their daughter, Belle, moved to Mars to become farmers. They work hard to grow crops and hybrid animals suitable for life on Mars. But farm life is hard. Wolves prowl the night, and Water Raiders are a constant threat to farmers' most valuable resource. Winters are especially long and harsh. Temperatures often plunge to 10 degrees below zero or more. Families usually take shelter in their underground homes to wait for spring to arrive.

The Song family has survived their first winter on Mars. Now spring is in the air. Temperatures are warming, the land is thawing out, and the Songs are going on a trip to the capital – Tharsis City. What wonders await Belle and her family as they visit Tharsis? And what dangers might lurk on the streets of the most wondrous city on . . .

REDWORLD

CHAPTER ONE
A SURPRISE

Belle watched her father, Yun, as he installed the computer panel over their brand-new water tank. Last autumn, Water Raiders had destroyed the Song family's underground tank. The entire field where the tank lay had been scorched by fire. Over the winter, the land had frozen over, so that no work could be done on repairing the tank. Thankfully, the neighbouring farmers were kind and generous. They helped provide for the Songs' water needs during the long winter.

As soon as spring arrived and the ground thawed out, Yun began working to install a new tank. Again, their neighbours had come to help. Belle wasn't strong enough to do much of the work. And Belle's mum, Zara, hadn't been feeling well for several weeks. However, their Personal Home Helper android, Melody, was very useful. She was especially helpful when it came to communicating with the computer that controlled the tank and its pump.

Belle crossed her fingers and held her breath as her dad prepared to switch the pump on. Her friends, Lucas and Ta'al, watched near by as Yun hopefully made his final attempt at turning on the pump. Yun had already made several attempts. But the pump had failed. Twice in the last week the alarm that told them the pump had gone offline had triggered for no reason. It once went off in the middle of the night, waking the Songs from their sleep and scaring them half to death.

"Here we go," Yun announced. He flicked the switch.

There was a moment of complete silence. Then the pump came to life, humming smoothly. It was a good sound. Everyone cheered.

"Third time lucky, or so the saying goes," Lucas said with a laugh. Lucas Walker was Belle's first friend when she'd arrived at the farm. The Walkers were their closest neighbours. Paddy and Myra Walker had been a great help to Yun and Zara when they first arrived and still had much to learn about farming. Myra was part Sulux, the alien race that helped humans to terraform Mars more than two hundred years ago.

"That's an odd saying," Ta'al said. "I don't believe there's any mathematical proof of its truth." Ta'al was Belle's best friend. She was very clever, but sometimes took things too literally. Ta'al was Nabian, another alien race that lived on Mars alongside humans. There were several alien races that made Mars their home, but Belle had only met Sulux and Nabians.

"Well, so far, so good," Yun said, turning to Ta'al's parents, So'ark, He'ern and Fa'erz. Nabian parents came in groups of three. "And your gift of the extra security system will certainly help us to sleep better at night. We can't thank you enough."

Nabians were the most ancient and advanced race that lived on Mars. After the wave of Water Raider attacks the previous autumn, Ta'al's parents offered to share their security technology. The Songs couldn't have asked for a better gift. A secure water tank was a necessity for an Olympian farmer. Without water, none of them would survive.

So'ark crouched by the tank's control panel. She made a few adjustments to the security program.

"You are most welcome," she said. "We can share this technology with all of our neighbours, if they desire it."

Paddy Walker slapped his thigh. "Well, that'll certainly help us keep those pesky raiders away. Thank you!" He spoke very loudly, all the time, as if everything he said was important. Belle liked him.

He'ern, Ta'al's father, was watching near by. He nodded his agreement and nudged Fa'erz. Fa'erz was their third *elixian*, or equal partner, as Ta'al had explained it to Belle.

Fa'erz pulled out a palm-sized disc. "I will make a note to download our technology for the Walkers' farm."

The Nabians' tall, lean bodies swayed like trees in a light breeze as they watched So'ark tweak the tank's control panel. Belle knew this meant they were a little nervous. They'd been worried that their technology would not work with human technology. So'ark had spent all winter trying to fix that problem. And now they would test it together on the security system.

"It's ready," So'ark said, rising to her full height and towering over Belle's dad. "Try it now."

"Here we go again," Yun said. He entered the passcode that So'ark had given him.

An energy field, that reminded Belle of a bubble, rose around the perimeter of the underground tank. The energy field's reflective surface glistened in the bright spring sun as it grew to meet in the middle. When all the sides touched in the centre, the shield sizzled. It sounded exactly like a turken leg being thrown onto a barbecue grill.

"Go ahead," So'ark said to Yun. "Try touching the force field."

Belle gaped at So'ark. She didn't like that idea. Why would So'ark encourage her dad to touch something that was meant to keep the bad people away? Wouldn't he get hurt? He'd already been stunned once before when raiders had attacked their farm. She remembered how frightened she'd been seeing her dad unconscious and lying on the ground. She didn't want to see him hurt again – or ever.

Yun gave her a mischievous grin and stuck his hand into the shield. "Aaggh!" he yelped loudly, and began shaking like a rag doll in a dog's mouth.

"Dad!" Belle screamed. "Help him!"

Yun pulled his hand out of the shield and burst into laughter. "I'm fine, Belle! I was just teasing. But it's amazing. I can't reach in far enough to touch the tank."

Belle glared at her dad. "That's not funny!" She couldn't believe he'd tricked her.

He wiped a tear from his cheek and cupped her face in his hands. "I'm sorry. But I couldn't resist. The look on your face was totally worth it."

Belle squirmed out of his hold. "Stop it. I'm not a baby." She hated that her dad always treated her like she was a child. She was thirteen after all.

Her face was hot and everyone was watching her. She disliked being put in the spotlight and wanted to hide. Ta'al came to her rescue.

"It looks like the shield works," Ta'al said. They watched as the energy bubble settled flat over the surface of the tank. It made a sucking sound, as if it had vacuum-sealed itself to the water tank. Turning to face Belle, Ta'al said, "Why don't we go and finish off our science fair project?"

Belle took a deep breath and swallowed the irritation she was feeling towards her dad. She nodded, but couldn't speak just yet. She was still fuming from her dad's silly prank. But she also remembered that Nabians treasured good manners, so she pushed her feelings aside to thank Ta'al's parents.

"Without your help, our farm would not be a safe place," Belle said in Nabian. She had learned the correct words and gestures from Melody, her android. Melody had researched Nabian expressions of gratitude just for this occasion. This morning Melody had gone into Sun City with Belle's mum, Zara. But Belle remembered what Melody had taught her.

"Your generosity is more than we deserve. *Sia-mi* – thank you." Belle rolled her hands around in a dance-like movement, a Nabian expression of thanks.

Ta'al's parents clapped when Belle had finished.

"How thoughtful of you to learn our ways," He'ern said, returning the hand gesture. "You honour us."

Belle looked over at Ta'al, who was beaming. Even Yun looked impressed by his daughter. It made Belle feel better, just a little.

The sound of hooves told Belle that her mum had returned. Zara hadn't been feeling well, so Yun had insisted that she go to the doctor in Sun City for a check-up. Their horsel, Loki, was pulling the Songs' hover wagon up to the house. The huge half-horse, half-camel creature neighed when he came to a stop. Melody stepped out of the wagon, carrying some supplies for the week. Zara climbed down slowly. She looked pale, but Belle thought she detected a smile on her mum's face.

Zara handed the reins to Belle, who unhitched Loki from the wagon. Together with Ta'al, she led him off to his stable to feed him. When Belle opened the stable doors, her dog, Raider, came bounding towards her. His one chewed-up ear, the result of a previous fight with another dog, flopped to one side.

"There you are!" Belle cried. "Were you sleeping in Loki's stable all this time?" Raider was a wolf-dog hybrid that Belle had adopted.

"You know, a year ago I wouldn't have believed that I'd be taking care of animals this size," Belle said to Ta'al. "It's hard to believe I used to be afraid of them."

"I still am," Ta'al said nervously, keeping her distance. Most Nabians weren't fond of animals, and they didn't keep pets. But Ta'al tried to be accepting of Raider.

When Belle had finished settling Loki, the girls headed back to the Songs' underground home. Martian farmers lived under the surface because of the planet's harsh weather conditions and dust storms. Even in spring, when the weather was warmer, dust storms could occur at a moment's notice.

"So, what did the doctor say?" Belle heard her dad ask her mum as the girls entered the small kitchen. Zara was putting away the supplies. Melody was helping her.

"Would you like me to project the physician's report?" Melody asked, turning to Belle, Yun and their guests.

"No," Zara said abruptly. Her face was flushed. Belle was puzzled. It was a little crowded but it wasn't that warm inside their house. Was her mother seriously ill?

"Perhaps we should leave," So'ark suggested. "Ailments are a private matter to humans."

Zara laughed nervously. "It's not that. I can scarcely believe it myself." She moved to the living room and sat down. A strange look of disbelief crossed her face. Yun looked worried, which made Belle even more worried.

"What is it, Mum?" Belle asked, sitting next to her.

Zara took Belle's hand. She looked at her and then at Yun. "It's a nice surprise, really," she said. "Our family is about to get bigger."

Belle looked from her mum to her dad. It took a few seconds for the news to sink in.

"You're going to be a big sister, Belle!" Yun exclaimed. He hugged Zara as their friends gathered around to congratulate her.

"How do you feel?" Ta'al asked Belle a few minutes later. "Nabians rarely have more than one child. I've often wondered what it would be like to have a sibling."

Belle wasn't sure how she felt. "I don't know," she said. "I suppose it's good news. And I'm old enough to help take care of a baby. It could be fun."

"You're going to be busy helping your mum," Lucas added. "That's what I hear from other kids anyway."

"Should we not tell them about the physician's advice?" Melody asked after all the congratulations were over.

Zara shook her head. "It's nothing," she said. "The doctor suggested that I see a specialist in Tharsis City. Because this is my first pregnancy on Mars, she thinks that a more complete check-up is necessary."

"The differences in atmosphere and gravity sometimes cause complications for humans in this condition." Melody spoke with such authority, it alarmed Belle a bit.

Zara laughed at how seriously the android put it. "It's not that bad. Besides, Tharsis is so far away, and we can't leave the farm for that long. I'm sure I'll be fine."

Yun took his wife's hand. "Nonsense. We've been cooped up all winter. We deserve to take a break. A visit to the capital is just what we need. I say we should make it into a short holiday. What do you say, Belle?"

"That would be great!" Belle said excitedly. School wouldn't start for a couple more weeks. And they really had been cooped up all winter. A trip to the city would be a welcome change from the boring chores and routine of the last several months. "Can Ta'al and Lucas come too?" she asked.

Ta'al looked up at her parents, who spoke with each other in their language.

"We're expecting Paddy's family to visit in a few sols," Myra said. "It's their annual holiday with us."

Lucas looked disappointed.

"Maybe next time," Zara said, smiling at Myra.

"We have never seen the capital," Fa'erz said. "If you have no objections, we would like to join your expedition."

Belle jumped for joy.

"I'm not sure I'd call it an *expedition*, but we'd welcome the company," Yun said, laughing. "It'll be fun. We'll camp in our wagons, and in two days, we'll be in Tharsis City, capital of Olympia."

Zara insisted that everyone stay for dinner to celebrate the good news. Melody cooked a meal combining Nabian spices with roast turken and lots of vegetables. Zara didn't eat much. She still looked pale, but she seemed happy. And that made Belle happy too.

I'm going to have a baby brother or sister. I've never thought about our family as being more than the three of us — and Melody, of course. I suppose it could be fun. I just hope Mum will feel better soon. Having a baby seems like a lot of trouble to me.

I'd rather think of our road trip! I can't wait. Tomorrow, we're heading out to Tharsis City. I'm so happy that Ta'al is coming too. It's too bad Lucas couldn't come along.

I looked Tharsis City up on the map. It's a long journey by wagon, but we can't afford to take a shuttle. We'll travel closer to the three volcanoes and Mount Olympus than I've ever been. Olympus is the largest volcano in the whole solar system! Also, we'll be crossing the Marine Valley River and Dad says we might stop and visit a desalination plant.

I wonder what Tharsis will be like? In the holo-vids it seems like an amazing city of the future. When we landed on Mars I saw a bit of Utopia, the capital of Eastern Mars. It was big, but it didn't seem as grand as Tharsis.

I really need to get some sleep, but I'm too excited!

CHAPTER TWO
:ROAD TRIP:

The next morning, Melody had the wagon packed and
ready to go before anyone got out of bed.

"What would we do without you?" Zara asked Melody
as she wrapped a warm blanket around half-asleep Belle.

"A day without an android is like a day without food."
Melody was trying out one of her bad jokes. "You'd survive,
but it would be most uncomfortable."

"Ugh, that's awful," mumbled Belle. "It's not even a joke, really."

But Zara laughed anyway.

"I am still in the process of learning about humour," the android said. "Your mother was amused."

Leaving before dawn meant that they'd be able to camp right next to the Marine Valley River later that night. But being up so early was hard for Belle. She grumbled all the way to the wagon, climbed inside, and fell straight back to sleep in her bed. Raider lay on the floor by her side, and she could hear his soft panting as she drifted off. Even Loki's whinny and odd gait didn't wake her.

Belle didn't wake up again until the sun rose and shone down on her through the wagon window. Melody was still charging in her portable station when Belle blinked her eyes open. She felt something weighing down her feet. When she sat up, she saw Raider asleep at the end of her bed, snoring quietly. He stirred when she moved. She scratched his ears and wiggled her feet out from under him. Slipping out of her bed, she tiptoed to the front of the wagon where her parents sat to guide Loki on the journey.

"Where will we meet up with Ta'al's family?" Belle said, stifling a yawn.

"They said they'd meet us at the campsite tonight," Yun said. He checked the navigation system. "That should be sometime this evening. We're gaining a lot of time with Loki's speed."

"You should probably have a wash and get dressed," Zara said. She looked pale but seemed cheerful.

Dressing in a moving hover-wagon was harder than Belle expected. And with Raider constantly nudging his head under her hand for attention, it took Belle longer than usual to get ready. When she sat down to breakfast, the dog laid his head on her lap and stared at her with his large brown eyes. He whined a few times.

"What is it, boy?" she asked.

"Perhaps he needs to go outside," Melody said, as she unplugged herself. "He has been indoors longer than usual."

When Belle asked her dad to stop, he reluctantly pulled over to the side of the road. Belle opened the back door to the wagon, and Raider jumped out before she could blink.

"He must really need to go," she said, following him outside.

Melody climbed down too, ready to go with Belle.

"Melody, wait!" Yun called. "I think something has come loose under the hover-wagon. I could use your help to fix it."

"I'll be fine," Belle said, waving off her android. "We won't go far."

Raider stopped at the first bush he found and relieved himself. Belle breathed in the cool morning air, glad for the chance to get out and stretch her legs too. She picked up a stick and threw it for Raider several times. Each time, he brought the stick back and wagged his tail for more. He even barked a few times when she was distracted by the small stones at her feet.

"I could use some of these for my Petripuffs." Belle picked up a handful of colourful pebbles. Petripuffs were her own invention. The palm-sized balls were used for self-defence. When thrown at an enemy, the gel bubbles inside broke open and released a fine powder. When an enemy inhaled the powder, it paralysed them for at least thirty seconds. Last autumn, Belle had used her invention to help save Lucas from some vicious Water Raiders.

Raider's ears pricked up. Even his floppy, chewed-up ear stood straight up. He sniffed the air, cocked his head, and whined. He turned into the wind, and whined again.

"What's wrong?" Belle asked.

The fur around Raider's neck stood on end. A low growl rumbled from his chest. The sound sent a chill up

Belle's spine. She'd heard that sound before, when she'd first encountered wild wolf-dogs. Looking around, she saw nothing but a slightly raised hill, dotted with low bushes and a few scattered trees in the distance.

"Come on, boy," Belle said, patting his head. "We should get back inside."

Raider took a few steps away from Belle. Her heart skipped several beats. She was sure he sensed danger.

"Raider, come on," she called again.

He trotted off in the other direction.

"Raider!" She called out to him more firmly this time. "Come here."

Raider stopped in his tracks. He took a stance – back legs spread out, and ears flattened back against his head. He shifted his weight forward, lowering his body. Something in the distance, something Belle couldn't yet see, was approaching. Another low, warning growl vibrated through Raider's chest.

Belle held her breath.

One by one, a pack of five wild wolf-dogs appeared over the low hill. They had enormous heads and big muscular bodies. They stood only a few meters from Belle. They bared their teeth in a snarl and moved towards her.

But Raider had taken a stand, right between Belle and the wild animals.

Raider was crouched low and giving a warning snarl to the wild dogs. His fur twitched across his body as his muscles rippled, preparing for a fight. Belle had never seen him like this, and she couldn't tell which was more frightening – the pack, or her Raider trying to protect her.

For the longest time, the wolf-dogs stared at Raider, and he stared right back. Two of the wild dogs took a step closer to Belle. Raider adjusted his position, blocking their advance. Raider bared his teeth and barked several warnings at the pack.

Their wild, orange eyes shifted from Belle to Raider and back again. Belle could almost see them thinking about whether she was worth eating, especially if they had to fight Raider for her.

Raider took a step towards the pack. He threw back his head – and howled one long note into the air. What was he telling the pack?

Whatever it was, it seemed to work. Most of the wolf-dogs changed their stance. They seemed to relax and began to wag their tails. Two of the dogs whimpered quietly. A third even laid down. Raider seemed to relax too.

But the largest of the wolf-dogs decided that Belle was too easy a meal to pass up. As the rest of the pack took their eyes off Belle and Raider, the big one leaped at her.

Raider must have expected the move, however. As the big wolf-dog pounced, Raider jumped sideways and threw himself at the attacker. Raider's head connected with the wild dog's middle, sending him crashing sideways to the ground. The big wolf-dog let out a loud yelp of pain and shock.

The whole thing happened in the blink of an eye. Yet to Belle it felt like forever. She managed to squeal, alerting Melody. A moment later, Melody appeared by her side. A livestock prod stuck straight out of Melody's central cavity. Its electric blue tip sparked dangerously as it pointed at the pack of wolf-dogs.

The others in the pack whined pitifully when they heard the crackle of the livestock prod. They turned tail and ran, disappearing from view. The big one was still on the ground. His breath had been knocked out of him, and he struggled to get back to his feet.

Raider advanced towards him, barking madly. His eyes were bulging out of his head, and his fangs flashed in the sunlight.

This time, outnumbered and outmatched, the big wolf-dog decided Belle wasn't worth the fight. He lowered his head and backed away, never taking his gaze from Raider. At the top of the ridge, the big dog turned and ran off after the rest of the pack.

Raider straightened up. He shook his body as if he'd just been for a dip in a river. Then he trotted back to Belle, panting like nothing remarkable had happened.

Belle crouched down and gave him a big hug. "You saved my life!" she cried, burying her face in his fur. Her heart hadn't stopped racing yet, and his warmth was comforting.

"He is a good dog," Melody observed. "You were in great danger."

Belle stood up. "You won't tell Dad, will you?"

She looked over Melody's shoulder. The wagon was quite a distance away. It was a miracle that Melody had covered that distance in such a short time.

"How did you . . . ?" Belle pointed to the wagon.

"I was on my way to get you," Melody said, anticipating her question. "Your father is almost finished with the repairs."

Belle could see her dad as he emerged from under the wagon.

"I don't want Mum and Dad to worry," Belle said, looking at Melody. "We've only just started on our road trip. And Mum isn't feeling well. There's no sense in making things worse for her."

"I agree," Melody said. "But from now on, I go everywhere you two do."

Belle smiled. She was lucky to have two protectors. There was little chance of her getting into trouble on this trip. But she also couldn't wait to tell Ta'al all about how Raider had chosen to protect her against his own kind.

As they climbed back into the wagon, Melody paused. Her eyes turned blue.

"I am simply checking on the weather reports," she said. "It looks like we shall have a smooth journey to the campsite."

That suited Belle just fine. She climbed into the wagon after Melody. Raider jumped in behind them, and the family continued their journey towards the river. As soon as Belle fed Raider his breakfast, he curled up at the foot of her bed and fell asleep. His encounter with the wild wolf-dog had tired him out. Belle stroked his soft fur with one hand while she read some information about Tharsis City. They stayed this way for the next few hours.

"Do you know any wolf jokes?" Belle asked Melody, when she was tired of reading. She scratched Raider's ears as he slept. The wagon hovered smoothly under Loki's steady pace.

"What did the wolf say when someone stepped on his foot?" Melody was happy to indulge in her favourite activity – telling bad jokes.

Belle knew this one. "Aaoooooowwwww!" She laughed quietly, careful not to wake her dog.

"What did one wolf say to the other at a party?" Melody asked.

Before Belle could answer, Raider stirred. He sat up, as if something had changed. It took Belle a moment to realize that Loki's pace had slowed. Belle looked up towards the front of the wagon to see what her parents were doing.

"Look!" Yun said, pointing. A small cabin with a large holo-sign by it signalled the entrance to the official riverside camping area. The sky was beginning to turn pinkish orange. "We've arrived at the camp."

Yun slowed Loki down to a walk. They went through the registration booth, and then to the campsite that was assigned to them. Ta'al and her family had already arrived. They were just starting to cook dinner when the Songs pulled up beside them.

After a delicious meal, the two families enjoyed some time talking by the campfire and watching the stars. While the girls and Raider explored their campsite, the adults shared stories about life on their home worlds.

When it was time for bed, Belle and Ta'al begged their parents to let them have a sleepover. They agreed, and Ta'al slept in Belle's wagon that night. It was the first sleepover for both girls, and they stayed up and talked late into the night.

Sol 13/Spring, Mars Cycle 106

Ta'al and I are snuggled up on the floor of our wagon. She loved my story of how Raider had saved me. Funny, I didn't expect that Nabians would be so like humans in how they sleep. Ta'al and I talked for ages, and then she went silent. Instantly! She's completely asleep and looks so comfortable. I wish I could fall asleep that fast.

It's too dark to see the river, but I can hear it. It's loud, so it must be big. The sound of the water flowing is soothing. Dad says we'll try to visit the nearby desalination plant before we take the ferry across. But they don't allow animals inside, so Raider will have to stay in the wagon. I'm a little bit annoyed at that. Raider saved my life. He should be allowed to come with us. I hope he won't be too bored in the wagon, all by himself. Right now he's sleeping with Dad because Ta'al is afraid of animals. I can just hear his soft panting from inside my parents' makeshift room. I miss his soft furriness at my feet. Oh well, it's just for one night.

CHAPTER THREE
:DISAPPOINTMENTS:

The next morning Belle woke to Raider licking her face. She snuck him out of the wagon without disturbing anyone else. It was a bright morning, and the air was crisp. Raider chased Belle around and in between the wagons. They were both glad of the exercise.

The air here smelled different from the farm. Belle knew it was because of the salty water in the river. Mars' water was naturally salty, which was why the desalination plants were so important. The whole desalination process fascinated Belle. The way they worked to change the salty water to sweet, clean water, was science and technology at its best. She had watched every documentary that Melody could find about the plants. She couldn't wait to visit one later that morning.

By the time the sun had warmed everything up, Ta'al and all of their parents were finally ready.

"Come on!" Belle cried, growing impatient. "I read the plant's brochure, and they only take a certain number of visitors per day."

An hour later they reached the desalination plant. It was enormous! It was a towering, pyramid-shaped building with no windows. Huge pipes snaked around the building, leading to enormous tanks of water that surrounded the plant.

The building sat on a flat area overlooking the Marine Valley River. The river was so wide and misty that Belle could barely see the other side. The wind near the river was cold and strong. It almost knocked Belle and Ta'al over a few times as they tried to stay warm in their thin coats.

There were many visitors at the plant that morning, and the queue to buy tickets was long. While He'ern and Yun stood in the queue, the others found a bench under a large tree to wait. Belle noticed that a few visitors were Terrans. But most of the visitors were red-eyed Martian humans. After arriving on Mars, Belle had learned that Martian-born humans had a red ring around their irises.

Other tourists were Sulux, like Myra Walker. Sulux and Nabians came from the same planetary system, several light years from Earth. But they didn't always get along.

Belle knew that some people didn't like Nabians very much. So she wasn't surprised, only disappointed, when she saw the stares from others who passed their bench. Some smiled at Belle, but when they saw Ta'al and her family, their smiles turned to frowns. Once or twice, she even heard a Sulux say a word she didn't understand.

Ta'al and her family didn't hear any of it. Or at least they pretended not to. When Belle had had enough, she couldn't contain her questions anymore.

"Don't you get angry with people who are rude to you?" she asked Ta'al's mum. "They don't even know you and yet they treat you like an enemy."

Belle could tell that Ta'al was angry. Her friend was completely still and staring at the ground as if she was trying to burn a hole in it with her eyes. So'ark put a hand on her daughter's shoulder and looked at Belle.

"It is not our place to tell people what to think," she said in a low voice. "If they choose to be narrow-minded and ignorant, nothing we do or say will change that."

"We can only hope that they will eventually learn more about us and see that we all have a place on this planet," Fa'erz added. "The universe is far bigger and more diverse than any human can imagine. We must be patient."

"I couldn't do that," Belle said. "I'd rather yell at them to stop being so stupid."

So'ark smiled, but her eyes reflected the ground and not the sky, which Belle knew meant that she was sad. "Nabians are far more ancient than either Sulux or Humans. We must bear this burden of knowledge and wait."

"We will endure," Ta'al said, under her breath. So'ark patted her hand and nodded.

Yun and He'ern returned from the queue for tickets. They were both frowning.

"It looks like we won't be able to tour the plant today," Yun said with a grunt.

"The ferry terminal just announced that the next sailing will be their only one for today," He'ern said. "They are worried about the weather forecast for later in the day."

"We had to decide," Yun said. "We could stay another night in the camp and tour the plant tomorrow. But we thought it best to leave for Tharsis now and get there sooner. Besides, I think your mother would prefer to sleep in a real bed tonight, don't you?"

Belle couldn't believe it. They were so close to the plant, and she wouldn't be able to go inside? She felt the frustration grow in her chest, and her face grew hot.

Yun put his hand on her shoulder. "Maybe we can stop on the way back," he said. "There'll be plenty of opportunities to take a tour. Some other time."

Belle wanted to yell at someone. But Ta'al caught her eye. Her friend was disappointed too, and after what they'd just talked about, Ta'al had more reason to be angry than Belle did. But she was taking the disappointment with calm acceptance. Belle wanted to be more like her Nabian friend. So she took a deep breath, pressed her lips together, and just nodded. She was thirteen years old. She shouldn't behave like a spoiled child.

"Okay. But if we can't tour the plant," Belle said, trying to stay calm, "could Ta'al come with us on the ferry, at least?"

"I don't see why not," Yun said, looking to So'ark for permission. Ta'al's parents talked amongst themselves for a long time. When Ta'al came back, Belle could tell the answer was going to be no. Everything was going wrong. This trip was turning out to be a huge disappointment.

"I have to stay with my family when we get on the ferry," Ta'al said. "It seems Nabians have to go through a separate entrance. And we all have to stay together."

Belle didn't like this news at all. "That's not fair! How can they do that?"

"Those are the rules. I don't like it either, but there's no point in fighting it," Ta'al replied.

Belle wanted to fight it. That fire in her chest burned hotter. She hated that she couldn't do anything about the situation. She stomped into her family's wagon behind Raider and Melody. After taking her seat, Belle poked her head out of the window to wave to Ta'al.

"See you on the Tharsis side of the river," she called to her friend. She tried her best to sound cheerful.

Ta'al waved back, but she didn't look very happy either.

● ● ● ●

A little while later, a question kept lingering in Belle's mind. She turned to Melody. "I don't understand it. Why do the Nabians seem to get treated so badly by others?"

"A long time ago, Nabians refused to help terraform Mars, although they had the technology," Melody said.

Her eyes were green. She was accessing her archives. "They believed that humans should learn and create their own advanced technology. But the Sulux had no problem with simply giving their technology away. This caused a rift between the different races. It seems that many Martians have not forgiven the Nabians for their decision."

"That does sound a bit selfish," Belle said. She filled Raider's bowl with food and watched him attack it hungrily.

"Think about what you are doing now," Melody said. "You learned to take care of your turken chicks because Zara refused to let me help you. You hated them in the beginning, but you learned to be responsible. All that work taught you to care for bigger creatures with greater needs, such as Raider and Loki."

"Mum did say that if I could handle the smaller responsibilities, I could move on to more important tasks." Belle was beginning to understand. "So, the Nabians thought humans needed more maturity?"

"Precisely. But we will never know if the Nabians were right, because the Sulux helped humans make Mars livable anyway," Melody said. "Because much of that technology came from the Nabians, it caused problems between the two races. Still, without both the Sulux and the Nabians, humans would not be living on Mars today."

Belle tried to see all sides of the argument. But she couldn't decide who was right. Thinking about it made her head hurt. She left Raider to his meal, and went to sit at the front with her parents so she could see the ferry terminal as they arrived. Yun paid a small fee, and they waited while androids scanned their wagon.

"Their job is to make sure nothing dangerous is brought onto the ferry," Yun explained when he saw Belle's worried look.

"It's quite a long journey on the ferry," Zara said. "Even though this is the narrowest part of the river. If you look carefully, in the distance you can see the outline of the city on the other side."

Belle stood up on her tiptoes and squinted. Sure enough, she could just make out tall structures along the horizon. She couldn't wait to see the capital city.

Once they passed inspection, they moved on to another series of queues to wait for the ferry. A loud horn blasted through the air.

"This will be the only ferry of the day." The holo-image of a Martian man appeared in front of the waiting wagons, reminding them of what they already knew. "If you miss this ferry, please be back here tomorrow morning for the next ferry to Tharsis City."

"I'm glad we decided to skip the tour," Zara said, looking a bit ill. "I hope we make it onto this ferry."

Belle frowned. "I hope Ta'al's family makes it too."

She and her parents watched in awe as the giant ferry approached the dock. It was bigger than any shuttle she'd ever seen. It had fan-like propellers whirring on its surface, like a monster insect with many wings. It also had two huge hulls that, according to Melody, could cut through the water very smoothly.

"The propellers allow it to skim over the water in case of bad weather conditions," Melody explained. She had poked her head out of the wagon to watch the arrival of the ferry. "The main hover engine is below."

"We're lucky that the river is calm today," Yun said. "We should make it to Tharsis in plenty of time, if we get on this ferry." He counted the number of wagons in the queue in front of them.

"And because the water is calm, the ferry will be sailing as an ordinary sea-going vessel," Melody said. "It should be quite an experience."

The Songs were one of the last wagons allowed onto the ferry. Belle tried to find Ta'al's wagon, but there were too many other wagons to locate her friend. She crossed her fingers and hoped they had made it on board.

Once they were safely secured, packed tightly among hundreds of other wagons, another loud horn blasted through the air. This told the lucky passengers that they were pushing off and beginning to cross the river. Zara took the opportunity to nap. Belle, Yun and Melody took Raider for a walk around the ferry. Loki looked as though he was asleep at the end of the harness, like most of the other horsels around them.

The breeze from the river was strong but refreshing. Belle leaned against the railing while her dad held onto her. Raider trotted up to their side and stuck his head between the railings. He stuck out his tongue as if he was tasting the salty air. Melody stood with her arms and legs spread wide, as if she was daring the wind to knock her over. Belle thought it was the funniest sight she'd seen in a long time.

They watched the dark waves float up and down. As the ferry cut smoothly through the water, white moustaches of foam formed on the tips of the waves. Water stretched as far as the eye could see.

Only when they moved to the front of the ferry could Belle make out the skyline of Tharsis City. In the distance, beyond the city, the sky was dark, like a giant shadow. But right over the city, the sun was shining. It lit the city up, showing off its many red and grey buildings. Some of the tallest buildings glimmered in the sunlight. Belle's heart raced.

"Tharsis City looks like a fairyland from here," she exclaimed.

Yun laughed. "From what I've read, it is quite a city. It's the most impressive city on Mars."

Sol 14/Spring, Mars Cycle 106

Standing on the front deck of the ferry was fun, but my face froze after a few minutes. I loved looking out at the city as it grew bigger with each passing minute. It looks like an amazing place! We finally gave in when we couldn't feel our faces anymore and headed back to the wagon. Dad decided to take a quick nap with Mum. Raider is tired out from all the excitement. The hum of the ferry engines is quite hypnotic. But I can't sleep. I'm going to play 3D chess with Melody.

I can't wait to get to Tharsis City. I just hope Ta'al and her family made it onto the ferry too. The city won't be any fun without my best friend.

CHAPTER FOUR
:THARSIS CITY:

Belle was at the front of the wagon with her parents
as they drove off the ferry into the main city. Signs of
city life greeted them long before the city gates came
into view. Along the roadside, as each wagon passed
sensors, holo-banners popped up from the ground. They
advertised all sorts of wonders to be found in Tharsis.

Best Hotel in Town
Stay at the Desert Inn!

Topamei Medical Centre.
Most advanced medical facility on the planet!

Give your android a SPA day!
Restoration facilities available in many areas.

Have you tasted lab-grown steaks?
Give it a try at Borealis Planitia Steakhouse!

Belle gaped in awe as each banner popped up in front of them. She wanted to try everything they suggested.

"Just ignore the ads," Yun said. "We've already decided where we're staying and which hospital we're going to."

More and more banners popped up as they got closer to Tharsis. Belle eventually grew tired of them.

"There it is," Zara said as they rounded a small hill.

Belle gasped as Tharsis City came into view. Buildings taller than she'd ever seen, even on Earth, rose into the sky. The buildings were of all shapes and varying heights. Some looked like cylinders jutting up into the sky. Others were

shaped like prisms and slender pyramids. Several buildings had disc-like tops with many windows that looked like viewing galleries. Belle wondered what the view was like from such a high place.

The roar of a shuttle engine flying overhead caught her off guard, and she grabbed onto her dad's arm.

"Lots of air traffic here," he said with a laugh.

Belle looked up. The sky was dotted with aircraft of all shapes and sizes. Many were coming in low to land. A few smaller craft landed on top of buildings.

As they neared the city boundary, the level of noise surprised Belle. She had grown used to the stillness of the farm. Here the air was filled with a continual humming sound. Then there were the constant roars of engines, the clanking of wheels, horsels grunting and whinnying, and the continual chatter of hundreds of voices. These all gave Belle a chill of excitement.

As they came to the city gate, they were stopped for a short interview about why they had come to Tharsis City. Large silver and black androids with one red scanning eye, called Protectors, asked Yun several questions. They were tall and wide and scary to Belle. But after Yun had answered their questions, the Protector androids waved them through into the city.

Large signs floated out of the sky, declaring:

Welcome to Tharsis City
The Wonder of Mars!

The Songs had booked a room at the Starry Skies Hotel. It was one of the few places that allowed pets to stay with their families.

Their guidance system led them through Astronaut Avenue. It was a long street that was broken up by several crossroads. At each crossroad, they had to stop to allow other traffic to cross.

At each stop, Belle was amazed by the decorative shopfronts along both sides of the four-lane road. She swept her head back and forth, trying to take in the sights in every shop window. They passed a large toy shop that had all kinds of flying gadgets on display. Another shop sold the latest in home wares. Belle pointed out what looked like a self-cooking device to her parents. Fully prepared meals appeared within it every few seconds.

"I'd love to have that at home," Zara said, nudging Yun. "Melody and I would never have to cook again."

He laughed and shook his head. "Only if we won the lottery first."

At the seventh crossroad, they turned onto a smaller street – Starry Way. Loki slowed to a snail's pace as they searched for their hotel. Belle spotted a blue and silver sign floating above their heads:

Starry Skies Hotel
Sleep Among the Constellations

After checking in at the hotel reception, they took a glass elevator to their floor. Their room made Belle feel as if she were in the middle of a colourful cloud in space. The walls were swirled in pinks and purples, and artificial stars twinkled every few seconds.

"It's quite soothing," said Zara.

"And hypnotic," added Belle.

Raider wasn't sure about it, however. He barked at the fake stars whenever they twinkled. *Poor Raider*, Belle thought. She hoped he'd get used to the city and its strange sights and sounds. Otherwise this would be a miserable holiday for him.

As soon as they got unpacked and settled in their room, Yun suggested that they go out and explore the city.

"But Ta'al and her parents aren't here yet," Belle said. She didn't want to go out exploring without her friend.

"I'm sure Ta'al's family will turn up at some point," Yun said. "Come on, let's get some dinner. I'm starving." Even Zara was feeling hungry.

Tharsis City at night was just as busy as it was in the daytime. But it was colder. Belle was glad she'd brought along her coat. She even wrapped an extra scarf around Melody's neck.

As the Song family stepped out of their hotel, they were met by crowds of people hurrying from one place to another. The larger transports that were present earlier had now been replaced by smaller craft. Several of these were open-top carriages – some pulled by horsels, others by unseen engines. The noise level, though, hadn't changed at all. The city was still loud and unstoppable.

As they wandered about the city, Belle noticed that they were the only family walking with a wolf-dog and an android. She also noticed many Sulux and Nabians. They often acknowledged each other with a nod or a hand gesture of greeting. Belle was surprised. The two races seemed to be a lot friendlier to each other in Tharsis than at home.

Belle was also surprised at how many other alien races were here too. The first person they met was the driver of a horsel-drawn carriage. He, or she (Belle couldn't really tell), offered to show them the city for a rather steep price.

"He is Parsiv," Melody told the Song family as they were approached. "They come from a star system very far from here. There are not many Parsiva on Mars."

The Parsiv made a sound, as if he were singing. Belle was puzzled.

"That is the Parsiv way of saying welcome to visitors," explained Melody. "I downloaded the more common languages in Tharsis into my memory banks. I thought it would be helpful."

"It is," Belle said. She smiled and waved at the Parsiv carriage driver.

"Welll-coome!" He said the word like it was part of his greeting song.

The Parsiv had a long, narrow face with three eyes. His four arms ended in hands that looked like fins with very fine skin. "See the night lights by rrr-omantic ca-rrr-iage. I have many blan-kets to keep you warrrm."

The Parsiv driver emphasized the 'r' in his speech. He sounded a little like a purring kitten. Belle liked him instantly and was sorry that they couldn't afford a ride.

Suddenly the air was filled with the blaring of an alarm. The carriage driver's horsel whinnied, and Raider barked. Belle had heard alarms like this before, back in Sun City. It meant that everyone had to run for cover, preferably underground. Belle couldn't believe it. A dangerous dust storm was coming – here in Tharsis City!

CHAPTER FIVE

:UNEXPECTED:
SURPRISES

She looked to her parents. They looked almost as nervous as she felt. The carriage driver, on the other hand, just shrugged. He stroked his horsel with his two fin-like hands to calm it.

"Where should we go?" Yun asked him.

The alien nodded. "Ah yes. You arrre new to Tharrrsis." He pointed to the sky. "Watch."

Looking up, Belle watched as an energy bubble grew across the sky above them.

"It's just like the new security system over our water tank!" Belle exclaimed.

Sure enough, the bubble grew until it formed a dome that covered the entire city. Other people in the streets stopped and watched the shield form as well. For a moment, the city was quieter than it had been since Belle arrived. Once the shield was complete, everyone continued going about their business.

"Tharrrsis is prrro-tected," the alien carriage driver said. "No worrries. Enjoy yourrr stay."

"That is incredible," Yun said, as they made their way to Astronaut Avenue. "It must be Nabian technology."

"It must use a lot of energy," Zara said.

Melody confirmed Zara's guess, but the numbers went right over Belle's head. Within minutes, the dust storm hit the shield. It sounded like distant thunder that never stopped. Belle and her parents found a bench and sat down to watch the storm as it swept over the city. Raider crawled under the bench and whined quietly. He didn't understand what was happening.

"This is such a rare opportunity," Yun said. "To see a storm up close and not be harmed by it."

"Indeed," Melody said. "There is only one other shield like this on Mars. It is in Utopia. Tharsis City must be very important to have expensive technology such as this."

Belle was mesmerized by the storm, until she realized that her friends might be out there in it.

"Ta'al and her family!" she cried. "What if they're stuck outside the city?"

Zara gasped. "That's right! I hope they're okay."

"Don't forget," Yun said. "They're Nabian. They're probably better prepared for storms than most of us."

Belle hoped her dad was right. She didn't like the idea of her friend being out in this storm.

After about ten minutes, Belle became bored with watching the storm. And her stomach was growling. The Songs continued their walk to find something to eat.

"Look who we've bumped into!" Yun cried, as they crossed Astronaut Avenue.

Parked in front of a large shop called Sol's was Ta'al's family's wagon. So'ark and He'ern jumped down as soon as they saw the Songs. Ta'al ran up to Belle.

"We've had quite an adventure," Ta'al said with a big grin.

"Indeed," So'ark said, coming up behind her. "We misunderstood the ferry queuing system. We thought the Nabians were being sent to the end of the queue."

"Instead, we were allowed on the ferry ahead of others," He'ern said. He flapped his long sleeves, straightening out his robes.

"Apparently, in Tharsis City, as in Utopia, Nabians are given extra privileges," Fa'erz said. "We arrived late because we were given a tour of the city's power grid."

Ta'al pointed at the shield above them. "It uses Nabian technology. Tharsis authorities are so grateful for it that all Nabians are treated to a free tour of how they use it." She spoke quickly and excitedly. She took a deep breath. "That's why we're late."

Belle was pleased for her friend. Tharsis seemed like a good place for people from all planets to live. She wanted to hear all about her friend's adventure, but right now she was too hungry.

"Well, you couldn't have arrived at a better time," Yun said, clapping He'ern on the back. "We were just looking for some dinner."

Not far away they found a traditional Nabian restaurant. Ta'al seemed excited by this so they all went in. The Nabian hosts greeted them all in the usual way. But the main host kept glaring at Melody and flicking his chin in her direction. He said something to Ta'al's family in their own language.

"I think I should wait outside," Melody said.

"Why?" Belle asked.

"They do not allow androids inside."

So'ark looked embarrassed. "We apologize. We could go elsewhere."

"It's all right," said Yun. "Rules are rules." He told Melody to go back to the hotel and wait in the room.

"You might as well take Raider with you," Zara said. "I'm not sure they'd like a big hairy wolf-dog in their restaurant either."

Belle tried not to show her displeasure. Melody and Raider were a part of their family and she didn't like to exclude anyone.

Dinner soon made her forget her bad mood. She was famished, just like everyone else. And the food was delicious. Melody's Nabian food wasn't nearly as good as this.

After dinner, the two families walked down the street, looking for dessert. They found a small shop that sold frozen sweets. The shop assistant was another type of alien Belle hadn't met yet. She watched as he folded several flavours together with his four arms, creating a colourful and edible flower. Belle didn't want to ruin it by eating it, but she couldn't resist. As she took a bite, all the flavours burst in her mouth with the most amazing sensation.

"I'd eat this every day if I could!" she declared. She and Ta'al slurped their special desserts as they walked back to their hotel.

At the hotel, the Songs waited for Ta'al's family to check in, and then returned to their own room. When Yun opened the door, Belle expected Raider to bound out to greet her. But the room was completely silent.

"Raider? Melody?" Belle called.

There was no response.

She walked through the room. As the automatic lights came on, she realized that the room had been untouched since they'd left for dinner.

Yun called down to reception to ask if anyone had seen Melody and Raider return. But nobody had seen either of them.

Belle felt sick. All that food she'd eaten threatened to come back up again. Her heart raced, and she felt cold and hot at the same time. What had happened to Melody and Raider? Where could they be?

Sol 14/Spring, Mars Cycle 106, evening

I can't sleep. Dad went out again to look for
Melody and Raider. He wouldn't let me go with
him. But I hate waiting in this room. I keep
thinking about the kind of trouble they could be
in. They'd be expecting me to come to their rescue.
Mum said she's worried too but she's fast
asleep now. So it's just me in this room, all alone.
If anything happens to either of them, I don't
know what I'll do.

Sol 15/Spring, Mars Cycle 106, past midnight

Dad came home empty-handed. He said that
Tharsis City has a midnight curfew whenever
there's a storm. He had no choice. He promised
we'd try again in the morning.

CHAPTER SIX
:MISSING!:

Belle was the first to wake the next morning. She could barely wait for her dad to get ready so they could look for her missing friends.

"We have to take Mum to the hospital for her check-up first," he said. "Then we'll set out to look for Melody and Raider. I've already reported them missing to the authorities."

Belle stomped her foot and was about to shout at her dad, but then saw how pale her mum looked. She was torn. She desperately wanted to find Raider and Melody, but she was also worried about her mum.

"Melody is resourceful," Yun said to comfort her. "And Raider has a great sense of direction. I'm sure he'll find his way back to us."

Belle was afraid her android and dog could be in trouble, and that someone might have harmed them. To say it out loud would've made it impossible for Belle to get through the day. So she pushed the thoughts to the back of her mind and went quietly with her parents to the clinic.

The hospital was only a few streets away. Zara was feeling weak, so they walked slowly across Astronaut Avenue, and turned down Main Street. Then they looked for Healthcare Avenue. Belle took the opportunity to ask everyone they passed if they'd seen Melody or Raider. She walked into one shop that sold antiques. All kinds of ancient things were stacked almost to the ceiling. She showed the shopkeeper a holo-image of Raider and Melody. But the Martian lady shook her head sympathetically.

Most people Belle met didn't believe that Raider was tame and worried that a wild animal might be loose in the city. Belle had to convince them that he was safe.

"If you see him, please contact me at this hotel," she said to an alien working in a shop that sold holo-vid programs. "If you feed him mealworms, he'll stay with you. He won't hurt anyone, I promise."

Belle had expected people to be uneasy about looking for a wolf-dog. What she didn't expect was the negative attitude people had about Melody. Most people didn't seem to care that she was missing. It didn't seem to matter when Belle told them how much Melody was loved by her family.

"We don't need androids that try to be human," one shopkeeper said. "Not after what happened on Earth."

Belle couldn't believe people were still afraid of something that had happened so long ago. How could she convince them that Melody was her best friend?

At the hospital, Belle sat in the waiting room while her parents went in to see the doctor. After half an hour of waiting alone, Belle became restless. She began exploring the hospital. Soon, she found herself standing outside the main entrance. As people arrived at the hospital, she showed them holo-images of Melody and Raider.

"Have you seen my friends?" she asked.

Most people were kind enough to look, but all shook their heads. No one had seen either a wandering android or a big wolf-dog.

Then one elderly Martian stopped and stared at the holo-images for a lot longer than the others.

"Hmmm, that chewed-up ear . . ." the man said, thoughtfully rubbing his chin.

"Yes?" Belle said. This was the first person to even think about Raider's appearance. Her heart raced. "He's always had this one strange looking ear. My Dad thinks he may have been injured in a fight with another wolf-dog before he lived with us."

The man nodded. "I heard someone say something just like that last night."

Belle bounced up and down. She was finally getting somewhere in her search. "Please, can you tell me where you heard that?"

"I believe it was last night, at dinner," he said, staring at the image of Raider. "There's an old diner just down this street."

He squinted in the direction he'd just come from. "I went there for a bite to eat last night. I have to stay near the hospital, in case my wife needs me. She's not well, you see. Anyway, there were three men at the table behind me. They were loud, and I couldn't help but overhear them. It isn't polite to listen in on other people's conversations, you know?"

Belle grew impatient. She wanted to tell the old man to just get to the important part – where was Raider? But at the same time, she was afraid to interrupt him. This man had her only clue to Raider's whereabouts.

"What were they saying?" she asked, as politely as she could manage.

The man looked up at the hospital as he thought about the previous evening. "One of the men, the loudest one, was bragging that he'd found a new dog. He was talking about the dog having a chewed-up ear and how he must have been in a fight in the past. It seems similar to what you said about your dog. Maybe it's the same one."

The man looked back down at Belle and rubbed his chin again. "I could be wrong, I don't know," he finished.

"No, I think you're right!" Belle said, a little too excitedly. "I think that's my dog he was talking about. His chewed ear is very distinctive. Can you describe what the man looked like for me?"

The old man nodded. "He was still bragging about how strong this dog was when I got up to leave. I remember that a Protector walked into the diner, just as I left. It was strange because the men at the table went completely silent. Their sudden silence made me turn to look at them."

Belle could barely contain herself. "What did this man look like?" she repeated.

"He was big," the man said. "He had messy, dark hair and a fuzzy beard. He wore several layers of clothing. Seemed a little dangerous to me."

It wasn't much of a description, but it was the most she'd received all day. Belle asked for directions to the diner, then thanked the old man and took off running. She knew she should have waited for her dad, but she didn't want to lose the only clue she had.

I'll find out more at the diner, and then come back and tell Dad what I've learned, she told herself.

The diner was called The Dirty Shoat. A hologram of a big, horned shoat rolling around in some dirt glowed on the outside of the door. Without another thought, Belle pushed open the door.

The foul smell of old cooking oil and sweat hit her right in the face as she walked in. She tried not to gag. It was a bright morning outside, but only a few streaks of sunlight made it through the grimy windows. The whole place looked dingy, old and dirty. There were only a few people inside – most of them were sitting at tables. One man leaned heavily against a counter inhaling the steam from whatever was in his large cup.

An odd-looking android rolled back and forth behind the counter. It was cleaning the counter with a cloth, stopping once to refill the customer's hot drink. This android looked nothing like Melody. It had no head . . . only arms and a cylinder for a torso. It reminded Belle of a metal broom with arms.

They obviously don't want to interact with intelligent androids, thought Belle.

She showed the cylinder droid the image of Raider. She wasn't sure the android could see, but she had to try. "Did you overhear a large Martian with a beard talk about this dog last night? He might have mentioned a chewed-up ear."

The android stopped in front of Belle. The customer next to her looked over too.

"You are underage, with no adult supervision," the android said in a flat, robotic tone. "Children are not allowed to purchase goods on their own. Please return with an adult."

"I don't want to buy anything," Belle said, annoyed. She was old enough to enter a diner on her own. She hated that people treated her like a young child. Mum said it was because she was petite. She pressed on. "I was told a tall man with a beard was here last night. He was talking loudly about this dog. Did you see him? Do you know where he went?"

The android stopped in front of Belle. It scanned Raider's image with a green light that fanned out from the top of its body.

"The man you mention was here," it said. "His group became silent when the Protector entered. They left soon after."

"Yes, that's the one!" Belle was thankful for the old man's long story now. "Do you know where he went after leaving here?"

The man at the counter looked up from his cup. "Those men were labourers," he mumbled.

Belle turned to him. He took a long gulp of his drink, and then wiped his mouth with his sleeve. He blinked at her with tired, bleary eyes.

"They're the ones who built most of what you see in this city," he said. "They live at the old miners' camp on Sulphate Way."

"Where's that?" she asked.

The man rubbed his face and shook his head, just like Raider did after his encounter with the wild wolf-dogs. Her heart ached for her pet.

"The camp's at the edge of the city," the man said. He slurred his words, so Belle had to move in closer to hear him. His breath stank, so she tried hard not to inhale.

"It's unprotected from the weather," the man continued. "When a storm's coming, most of the people there seek shelter inside the dome. That's probably why they were here last night."

"Sulphate Way," Belle said to herself. She didn't want to forget that name.

Belle turned to leave the diner. But then a thought occurred to her. She turned back and showed the man another image of Melody. The cylinder droid was back behind the counter, and it scanned the image as well.

"Have you seen this android?"

"We do not serve androids," the simple droid said. "All unaccompanied androids are sent to the SPA facility."

"What's that?" Belle asked. She was sure it was not as relaxing as the name sounded.

The man at the counter blurted, "Humanoid robots get picked up by the authorities, especially if they're mucking around on their own."

"All unaccompanied androids must be taken to the SPA facility," the service droid repeated.

Belle walked out of the diner into the fresh air and bright sunlight. She squinted. She had two places to find, and had no idea where either one was. She needed help and knew just who to call.

Sol 15/Spring, Mars Cycle 106

I have to find the SPA facility and the miners' camp. But I don't know how to find these places. I usually rely on Melody to find that type of information.

I met my parents back at the hospital. Ta'al was there too with her parents. When I told them about the clues I'd found, Dad was awfully angry that I'd wandered off on my own. But he was glad to get the information about Melody. He agreed to go the SPA facility to get her.

Dad told me to stay with Mum while she rested back at the hotel. The doctor gave her some medicine to get over her sickness. But it's knocked her out. I can't just sit here in the hotel and watch her sleep, can I? Not when Raider's in trouble.

So I've talked Ta'al into sneaking out with me. I promised her we wouldn't do anything dangerous. I told her that if we found Raider, I'd call my dad right away.

I just hope we're not too late.

CHAPTER SEVEN

THE SEARCH FOR RAIDER

Ta'al downloaded an interactive guide map of the city onto her comm device. Together, she and Belle found where the mining camp was on Sulphate Way. This is where the man who had Raider probably lived. It didn't seem to be too far from the hospital. Ta'al started the guide program and a green arrow was projected onto the ground by their feet. It showed the direction they needed to go.

"Did you bring the Petripuffs?" Belle asked, as they crossed the street in front of the hospital. The arrow pointed to the right.

Ta'al patted her pockets. "We have plenty. And our new improvements should come in handy if we run into any trouble."

Belle shivered at the thought of meeting the large Martian and his friends. Her Petripuffs were really just a security blanket. They made her feel safe, but she hoped she'd never have to use them.

The streets were busy and crowded. Transports zoomed down the wide streets, kicking dust into the air. Impatient drivers rose above the ground to pass over other vehicles ahead of them. Drivers on the ground blasted their horns and swore loudly at those above them. It was chaotic. Crossing the streets on foot required a lot of courage. No drivers obeyed the pedestrian crossing signs. So the girls held hands and waited for an opening in the traffic.

"Ready . . . go!" cried Ta'al. The two girls dashed across the street as fast as they could. Ta'al was much faster than Belle. She barely kept up with her Nabian friend and was breathing heavily when they reached the other side.

The girls crossed two more main roads in the same way. Then the green arrow at their feet led them down pavements for several streets. Because there were so many tall buildings, the sun was hidden and they walked in cold shadow most of the time. Belle had to pull her thin coat snugly around herself and tuck her hands into her pockets to keep warm.

"This is Museum Walk," Ta'al said, reading the guide information on her comm device. "It says there are several historical buildings and artefacts here. Once Raider and Melody are safe, we should come back. It would be fascinating to learn more about the history of the city."

The girls kept following the green arrow on the ground. The traffic lights at the next junction were unlike the others they had seen. Not only were there lights warning people not to cross, but also barriers that rose out of the ground. The girls had no choice but to wait.

The ground began to rumble beneath their feet. Suddenly a large panel in the road slid open – and a train flew out of the underground! It was very long and fast, and it created a strong wind that blew the girls back a few steps.

"What is that?" Belle cried.

Ta'al tapped on her comm device. "It's the public transport train!" she said, shouting because the rumble got louder with each train car that emerged.

"It functions mostly underground up to this point. From here it continues on its route by hovering about three storeys above the ground." She looked up. "Amazing!"

After the train had completely emerged and the barriers were removed, the girls continued on.

As they passed one large window, Belle simply couldn't resist stopping to look. A salesperson was waving a wand-like device over some dull jewellery with boring grey stones. But as soon as the wand touched them, they came to life. The stones lit up in a wide range of colours and tiny holo-images popped up from each one. They looked like dancing fairies. Belle had never seen anything like it. She imagined her mum wearing such a necklace and how beautiful she'd look. The salesperson behind the window gave her an inviting smile, but Belle knew her family could never afford anything like this incredible jewellery.

"Come on, Belle," Ta'al called. "The arrow is blinking. Sulphate Way is just around the next corner."

The girls followed the arrow to the end of the street. At the corner, the arrow turned into a red circle. The sign above them showed that they had arrived at Sulphate Way.

"Which way now?" Ta'al said. "We don't have a full address, only the street name, so the guide program can't take us any further."

Belle tried to remember what the man at the diner had said. "We have to find a miners' camp. Maybe we should ask someone."

The girls stood on the street corner, trying to catch someone's eye. But people were walking by too quickly. No one made eye contact. Everyone just went about their business without acknowledging the two girls.

Belle decided to duck into the first building they came across to ask someone for information. It was a bank. The outside of the building looked like most of the other buildings in Tharsis – massive and reddish brown. Inside, however, everything was bright and shiny white.

"This is ancient marble!" Ta'al exclaimed, running her hand along the floor. "This kind of stone isn't found on Mars. They must have imported it from Earth. Amazing."

Belle had no idea what marble was, but it certainly was shiny. Their boots squeaked against the floor as they crossed the large reception to a high counter. Two droids that looked like Protectors stood at attention by the counter. A large, purple Sulux man stood on the other side. He looked down at the girls as if they were tiny bugs.

"May I help you?" he said. Then seeing Ta'al, he added it in her language. "*Kra-ni-toh-ku?*"

Ta'al giggled. "His accent is terrible," she whispered.

"We're looking for the miners' camp on Sulphate Way," Belle said, sounding more nervous than she felt. The wide space and brightness of this place made her appear small and scared. "Could you tell us where it is?"

The Sulux man stared at Belle for a long time. He pulled on his long, braided hair. "Why would a child such as you have business in a place like that?"

"My dog ran away," she explained. "And he was last seen there."

The man exhaled loudly and slowly. "If I were you, I'd report it to the Protectors and let them do their jobs. The mining camp is no place for a child."

That just got Belle's blood boiling. She glared at the man and stood as tall as she could. "I'm not a child."

The Sulux man shrugged. "Have it your way," he said, and then programmed the directions into their guide. The camp was at the very end of Sulphate Way.

"Thank you for your help," Belle said drily. Together the two girls dashed out of the building.

CHAPTER EIGHT
THE END OF THE ROAD

The closer they got to the camp, the more anxious Belle became to see her dog again. They picked up their pace.

Sulphate Way was a very long road. As they made their way along it, the buildings grew shorter and further apart. Fewer and fewer tourists walked along the street. It felt more industrial here, as if this area was where all the real work of the city was done.

Suddenly the pavement came to an end, as did
the roads. It was as if the city builders had run out of
material at this very spot. Over the girls' heads, they
heard a swoosh of wind. The hover-train ran all the way
out here, and disappeared into the encampment that lay
before them.

Across the dusty unpaved road, the girls saw a
rough stone wall with an ominous looking gate in the
centre. The wall surrounded a camp of large tents.
There were rows and rows of them inside.

"I suppose 'camp' was a literal term," Ta'al said,
sounding a lot like her mother.

Belle sighed. "How are we going to find Raider
in there?"

She wished more than anything that Melody were
with them. Her android would've been able to hear
Raider from this distance. Belle thought of all the times
she was rude to Melody and regretted every one of
them. She missed her friend. If she ever got Melody
back, she promised herself, she would treat her like a
precious jewel.

"I wonder if I can program this to emit a frequency
like a dog-whistle?" Ta'al said and began tapping on her
comm device.

The girls approached the gate slowly. Ta'al slowly waved her device back and forth as they moved forward. At the gate, they stood and listened. There must have been hundreds, even thousands, of people living inside. Voices filled the air, as well as the sound of animals – birds screeching, shoats bleating and dogs barking.

Belle's heart sank. The camp was like a huge maze. Without help, they'd never find Raider.

Ta'al groaned and tapped at her comm device again.

"I don't know what I was thinking," she said, frowning. "I can't reprogram my comm to do anything." She gave Belle an apologetic look. "And my parents are demanding we return to them."

"But, Raider . . ." Belle wouldn't budge. She gripped the bars of the gate tightly. They were sticky, and she didn't want to think about why.

"Belle, you promised we wouldn't do anything dangerous." Ta'al's voice rose. "If we don't go back now, our parents will never trust us again. We should go."

"When our parents find out what we did today, they're not likely to trust us anyway," Belle said sharply. She was frustrated. She was going to be in trouble for sneaking out. And worse, her sneaking hadn't produced anything useful.

Belle shook the gate to see if it would open. Two rough looking women walked by and glowered at her.

"A bit young to be coming for the fights, aren't you?" One of the women sneered at Belle.

Belle's heart jumped into her throat. "Wha- what fights?" she squeaked.

"If you don't know, then I'm not telling!" the other woman laughed.

Then the first woman charged at Belle, yelling something at the top of her lungs. Belle was so shocked, she couldn't move. The grubby woman grabbed onto Belle's hands, pinning them to the gate. Belle winced at the pain.

"Pretty little girls like you should stay away from places like this," the woman hissed. Belle leaned away because the woman smelled horrible, like old fish and something sour.

"I'm . . . looking . . . for my dog," Belle whimpered. She couldn't pry her hands away from the woman's grip.

The other woman watching from behind the gate laughed wickedly. "Your dog is likely gone, missy," she cackled. "Most of them don't survive a day in the ring."

And then as quickly as she had charged, the woman at the gate let go of Belle's hands. She hobbled away into the camp. The only thing Belle could hear was their mocking laughter and the pounding of her own heart.

"See? We can't do this on our own," Ta'al said urgently. "We need to get help."

Belle shivered. This wasn't a nice – or safe – place. But she was sure her dog was inside. And he was in danger.

Belle shook the bars of the gate again. But the gate wouldn't budge.

"Belle! Let's go!" Ta'al sounded desperate.

More people inside the camp passed by the gate. They were heading in the same direction as the two women.

"What fights are you going to?" Belle called out to them.

Most people ignored them and just kept walking.

"I'm leaving, Belle," Ta'al warned. "I'm telling your parents what you're trying to do." She tapped something into her comm device.

"Wait," Belle pleaded. "Let me just find out where they're going."

She called out to the people in the camp once more. "What fights?"

A younger man looked their way. He flicked his chin up at Belle and winked. He put a finger up to his lips. "Shh!" he said. "Don't tell now. We're heading to the dog fights!" Then he disappeared into the crowd.

Belle froze. She couldn't move a muscle. Her heart dropped, and she felt like she was going to be sick.

Dog fights?

The man who'd taken Raider was going to force him to fight other wolf-dogs? Or other creatures? Or even a person? Belle had no idea what a dog fight was, but she was sure it was the worst thing in the universe.

How was she going to save Raider? The gate was locked. She couldn't find a way in, and Ta'al was sending a message to tell her parents where they were. A fat tear rolled down the side of her nose and into her mouth. She felt Ta'al tug her sleeve.

"We need help," Ta'al said. "And if we tell our parents the whole truth, I'm sure they will come back with us."

Belle wasn't sure there would be time. She allowed her friend to take her hand and pull her away from the camp. It was as if all the strength in her body had flowed away. She couldn't stop thinking of Raider being bitten and scratched by another animal. She pictured him lying on the ground, injured, bloody and confused. She wondered if Raider felt let down by her. Did he think she had abandoned him to this horrid life?

Her mind was so full of thoughts about Raider that she didn't even realize that they'd arrived back at the hospital. She finally began to focus when she heard her dad's voice.

"And just where have you been young lady?" he demanded – loudly.

Ta'al's voice came next, and Belle knew she was explaining the whole story to him, but no words registered in her mind.

Her dad was yelling again. Belle didn't understand what he was saying, but he was clearly very angry. Still, she didn't care. Raider was in serious trouble, and she felt responsible. Without thinking, she wrapped her arms around her dad and began to sob, her tears soaking his light jacket.

Sol 15 /Spring, Mars Cycle 106, evening

I think my dad carried me back to the hotel.
I don't really remember much. I felt like such a
failure today. We went all the way to the mining
camp and couldn't do a thing. I can't stop thinking
about what might be happening to Raider.

I'm glad Ta'al was with me, though. She stays
so calm and positive. She's sure that we'll be able
to find Raider tomorrow.

Ta'al's mum gave me something sweet to
drink. She said it would help me to rest. She said
I'd need my strength tomorrow if we're all going
to save Raider and Melody together.

CHAPTER NINE

﹕AN ANDROID﹕
IN PIECES

The sky was dark outside by the time the Nabian medicine wore off. Belle heard low voices coming from the sitting area on the far side of the room. Yun and Zara were on the sofa, talking quietly.

"Have we found Melody?" Belle asked.

Yun nodded, without looking at Belle. "She's at a SPA facility not far from here."

"Then let's go and get her." This was the first good news Belle had heard all day.

"She's scheduled to be dismantled," Zara said, twisting her fingers together. "I'm so sorry."

"What?!" Belle cried. "We can't let them do that."

"They're not responding to my request to speak to them," Yun said.

"Then let's go to the facility." Belle couldn't understand why her parents hadn't thought of that.

"It's really late now," Yun said. "I'll send them a message to say we'll be there first thing in the morning." He began dictating a message into his datapad.

"NO!" Belle screamed. She hadn't meant to. The word had just come out that way.

She rushed to the door. "Dad, we have to go now. If they kill Melody, I'll never forgive you!"

"Melody can't be killed," Yun said, looking a little hurt. "The worst they can do is wipe her memory."

"Can't you see that's the same as killing her?" Belle cried. "Without her memories, she wouldn't be Melody!"

Zara nodded. "She's right, Yun. Melody belonged to my mother, and she has all the memories of my mother's life, my childhood and Belle's too. We can't let them reset her to nothing."

Belle stomped her feet. "You were the one who told Melody to go to the hotel on her own. This is your fault, Dad."

"Now Belle, that's not fair," Zara said, shooting Belle a warning look.

"But she has a point." Zara turned to Yun. "It wasn't your fault, but there's no harm in going to the facility now. We're all awake anyway."

Belle was so relieved that her mum was on her side. She looked over at her dad with tears in her eyes. Yun rose out of his seat and sighed. He picked up the coat that was slung over the back of the sofa.

"Come on, then," he said. "Grab your coat. Let's go and find our android."

After persuading Zara to stay and rest at the hotel, Yun and Belle rushed to the SPA facility. It was too far to walk, so they got into a tiny hover-cab. The driver was another cylinder droid, like the one in The Dirty Shoat diner.

"Dad, do you think they're going to turn Melody into one of these simple droids?" Belle couldn't bear to think of her friend without a head, legs or body with lots of secret compartments.

"Don't worry, Belle," Yun said. "We'll get there in time to stop anything bad from happening. Trust me."

Belle wished she could trust her dad. But she was so cross with him for not acting right away. This was turning out to be the worst holiday ever!

The SPA facility was another giant bulky structure. But this building had tall glass doors that opened into a bright reception area. Large letters lit up the wall in front of them as they walked in. It read:

Department of Planetary Protection:
Security Protocol for Androids.

"So that's what SPA stands for," Belle murmured.

People in blue uniforms walked about busily while staring at their datapads. Several cylinder droids rolled around on their wheels helping customers. One such droid rolled up to Yun and Belle.

"May I be of assistance?" it asked in the same flat, robotic voice as the diner droid.

Yun showed the droid Melody's order number, and it led them to a room at the back of the reception. There was a bench against the wall by a closed door with the number one on it.

"Please wait here," the droid said. "You will be served momentarily." Then it rolled away.

Belle fidgeted in her seat for several minutes. "No one is coming to help us," she grumbled.

Yun got up and went to ask another droid for help. It told him the same thing as the first droid. At the same time, a Nabian girl in uniform approached the door beside Belle. She tapped a pattern into the control panel and the door slid open. Belle got up to follow her.

The girl held up her hand to stop Belle. "Authorized personnel only. Please wait here," she said. The door closed.

"I have to do something," Belle said to her dad, as he sat back down. She looked around to make sure no one else was coming, then tapped the control panel and entered the same pattern the Nabian girl had used. The door slid open.

"Belle!" Yun followed her as she walked through the door. "You can't just barge in without permission. There are proper ways to do things."

Belle wanted to tell her dad that she rarely did things the *proper* way. Nothing would get solved if she did.

"You can't do this!" he whispered.

She looked up at her dad. "I just did."

The room behind the door was a laboratory. The lighting was bluish white and there were transparent pods in rows down the sides. Computers and robot parts sat neatly on counters and benches. A couple of workers were focused on android parts on the counters in front of them. More cylinder droids stood in the pods, probably waiting to be activated or repaired.

Belle tiptoed through the lab, searching high and low for Melody, but there was no sign of her. Her stomach twisted painfully. She began to look for robotic parts that might have been a part of Melody.

Then she found Melody's arms.

She squealed in fright, and the uniformed workers turned around.

"Hey! What are you doing in here?" a man asked. He rushed up to Belle.

Yun stopped the man before he reached Belle. "We're here to get our android back. Where is she?" He showed the man the holo-document with Melody's information.

"You should be waiting outside," the man protested, pointing to the door.

"We're not going anywhere until you show us where Melody is!" Belle yelled so fiercely that the man took a step back.

He looked at the holo-document once more and chewed on his lip.

"Fine," he said. "She's been cleansed anyway."

What does that mean? Belle thought, terrified.

The man led them to a bench along the back wall. Androids of all kinds were stacked in piles, completely dismantled! At the far end was a pile of parts where Melody's head sat on top. Belle wailed so loudly that everyone in the lab stopped to stare. She wrapped her arms around her android's head and glared at her dad.

"You did this!" she yelled. "This is all your fault!"

Yun's face went a deep red and his nostrils flared. He demanded an explanation from the man in the uniform. The man took Yun into a different part of the lab to see his supervisor, while Belle began to put Melody back together. The Nabian girl from earlier came along to help.

"I'm sorry this happened to your droid," she said. "I had a Home Helper when I was younger, and I really liked it too."

"Melody is more than a Helper," Belle said quietly. "She's my best friend."

The girl sighed. For the next few minutes they worked in silence, putting Melody back together. By the time Yun returned, Belle had Melody fully assembled.

"I need her memory chips," Belle said, afraid to look her dad in the eye. She knew in her heart that it wasn't his fault that this had happened. But she'd been so angry. Her mum was ill. Then she lost Raider. And now her oldest friend was in pieces. It was all too much to bear. She hoped her dad knew that she still loved him.

Yun opened his hand. He had Melody's chips in his palm. Belle inserted them into Melody's central processor, behind a panel in her head. Then she pressed the power switch on Melody's back. It took several tries before her eyes lit up a bright green. Melody turned her head left to right and back again. She stopped when her eyes met Belle's.

"Where am I?" she said. "What happened to me? The last thing I remember is . . ." she trailed off.

It wasn't a good sign. Melody should have recorded everything that happened up to the moment they powered her down.

"Do you know me?" Belle was worried that the SPA people had wiped her entire memory. Everything that they'd done over the years, all their adventures together, it would all be gone. Without her memories, Melody would be just another droid, like the ones rolling around this lab. Belle held her breath.

Melody's eyes scanned Belle. Then moved towards Yun and scanned him too. For the longest seconds in the universe, the android was silent.

"What did one wolf say to the other at a party?" she said at last.

Belle stared at her. Slowly, Belle's lips curled upwards into a smile. Then she laughed.

"We are having a howling good time," Melody finished.

"Have you completed your science fair homework, Belle?" Melody continued, standing up. She was a little wobbly. Belle tightened a few of her joints. She hugged Melody, squeezing her middle with all her might. Her android was back!

"I missed you so much," Belle said.

"And I have several hours missing in my memory, it would seem," she said.

The man who had caught them in the lab earlier returned with a holo-document. "It seems this droid was dismantled by mistake," the man said. "It's a 3X model, quite harmless. We apologize, but it's only a droid, after all."

Belle wanted to shout at the man. Melody was more than just a droid.

"Dad?" Belle said, as they walked back out into the evening air. "I'm sorry for screaming at you."

He put his arm around her shoulders. He was looking up at the stars that were beginning to appear in the clear, dark sky.

"I know how scared you were to lose Melody," he said. "I was too."

After finding a cab and climbing inside, Melody asked, "Where is Raider? The last time I saw him, he was growling at a large Martian man." Belle told her android about what had happened to Raider.

"We should go and find him then," Melody said.

"Oh, no," Yun said sternly, after giving their destination to the driver droid. "No more adventures for you two. We'll leave that to the authorities."

Belle looked at Melody. Melody's eyes turned blue. She was searching for information on Raider. Belle leaned over towards her android. "First thing tomorrow," she whispered.

"We will go in search of Raider," Melody whispered back.

Sol 15/Spring, Cycle 106, night

It's so good to have Melody home. She seems fine, but only time will tell if she's completely back to her old self. Ta'al's family was in our room with Mum, waiting for news. They were so happy to see Melody too. The more I get to know them, the more I love them.

Mum looked a lot better tonight. She laughed and chatted like her old self when she saw Melody. The only thing that I need now is Raider. Tomorrow, Ta'al, Melody and I are going to go find him.

Note to self... don't tell Dad.

CHAPTER TEN
A RISKY REUNION

As soon as Yun and Zara left for the hospital the next morning, Belle and Melody snuck out. Ta'al met them in the alley behind the hotel.

"I hate lying to my parents," Ta'al said. "But I know this is important."

Belle gave her friend a quick hug, and the three of them went off to rescue Raider.

"Wolf-dog fighting has been a problem in several cities on Mars," Melody said. "But Protectors have a hard time catching them in the act." She was still a little wobbly from being reassembled and walked more slowly than usual. Her eyes turned blue for a moment as she accessed the Tharsis City public database.

"Dangerous criminals run these fights," Melody continued. "The man you described may be one of the ring leaders. His name is Hans Punkin. There is an arrest warrant out for him. There is also a reward for his capture."

"A reward?" Ta'al said. "Is it a large one?"

Belle didn't care about any reward. The news about Hans Punkin meant that Raider could be in real trouble.

Finally they arrived at the end of Sulphate Way, and stopped outside the wall of the camp to survey the area.

Belle turned to Melody. "I thought you could scan for signs of Raider."

"That would be hard," Melody said, extending her neck joint upwards so she could scan the camp. "There are several wolf-dogs here. Raider does not have a distinctive voice. Nor does he have a tracker chip."

Belle's heart sank. She was sure that Melody would be able to find him.

"Wait. Look!" Ta'al exclaimed.

Ta'al pointed to where the wall turned the corner. Belle couldn't believe her eyes. A wolf-dog with a chewed-up ear was trotting out of another gate. It was Raider! He was being led on a short, thick rope held by a giant Martian man with curly hair and a messy beard. Melody scanned them both and confirmed that this was indeed Hans Punkin.

Ta'al gasped. "We have to do something. Call the Protectors now!"

"It's too late for that," Belle said. Without thinking, she ran forward.

Ta'al called out her name. "Belle, wait!"

"If we wait, Raider and Punkin will be gone!" Belle replied, charging towards her dog.

Raider must have sensed her coming. He stopped in his tracks and barked happily. The man glanced in Belle's direction and scowled.

He pulled Raider behind him. The dog yelped. " What in the . . . ? Are you the nosy kid who's been pestering everyone about me?" he roared, baring his ugly teeth.

Belle froze. Even from this distance, she could smell him. He smelled of old food and sweat. She gagged.

"I just want my dog back," Belle said, surprised that she wasn't at all afraid of the huge man. From behind him, Raider tilted his head to look at her.

Ta'al ran up beside Belle and secretly handed her two Petripuffs. Melody ambled up and stood at her other side.

"I've reported our situation," Ta'al whispered.

"*Your* dog?" the man growled. "I found him wandering the streets. He's a born fighter. I'm going to train him to be a champion. Go and play with your dolls and leave us alone."

Belle stepped forward. There was no way she'd let him turn her dog into a killer.

"The Protectors are on their way," Ta'al said. "You'll have no use for a dog when you're in prison."

"They haven't found me yet." Punkin spat at the girls. "And they never will." He began to march off in the other direction. He pulled so hard on the rope around Raider's neck that the dog's front feet rose off the ground.

"Stop that!" Belle shouted. She couldn't bear to hear the yelp that came from her dog. The big man was hurting Raider. She had to save him.

She charged forward. Holding her breath, she threw one of her Petripuffs at Hans Punkin. But he ducked, and the puff exploded behind him. He stomped towards Belle angrily, nostrils flared. He was so big, his body blocked out the sunlight. Belle was caught in his shadow.

"I'm gonna teach you a lesson, kid," he snarled.

He reached out and tried to grab Belle by the hair. She screamed and twisted out of his reach.

Then Belle heard a growl, low and sinister. Raider stepped between her and the giant man. The hairs on his neck rose and he growled again. Belle was afraid that Raider had turned against her. Punkin grinned.

"Told'ya so. He's a born killer," Punkin said.

Slowly, Raider turned to face the giant Martian. He gave a deep, warning bark, and locked eyes with Punkin.

"Shut up, you mutt!" Punkin ordered.

Raider dug his feet into the ground and held his stance. He lowered his body, just like when he had faced the wild wolf-dogs. His ragged ears perked up and he bared his teeth. He was ready for a fight.

The man looked at Belle and then at Raider. He seemed unsure if Raider would actually attack him.

In that moment of doubt, Melody stepped to Belle's side. She had produced the electric livestock prod stored in her chest compartment and pointed it at Punkin. He glared at Melody as the prod crackled in the air.

Before the android could do anything, Ta'al ran up and lobbed two Petripuffs over Raider. They hit Punkin's chest and exploded, spewing white powder into the air around him. He went as stiff as a plank and keeled over to land face

first in the dirt. Melody walked over and held her electric prod over the man's paralysed body.

Belle collapsed to the ground and gasped for air. She didn't realize that she'd been holding her breath the whole time. Raider trotted over and began licking her face. She wrapped her arms around his furry neck.

"I've never been so frightened in my life!" she cried.

"Neither have I," Ta'al said, sitting down next to Belle. "At least . . . not this season."

Belle looked at her friend and they both started to giggle. They didn't stop until the sound of drones above told them that the Protectors had arrived.

"I sent a quick message to my parents too," Ta'al said. "To tell them where we are."

"As always, you have saved us all," Belle said. Ta'al was the responsible one. Belle didn't want to think about where she'd be today without her sensible friend.

● ● ● ●

The next day, the Mayor of Tharsis City handed Belle's and Ta'al's parents the reward money for helping to capture Hans Punkin. She shook hands with Belle and Ta'al, and patted Raider on the head. She even smiled at Melody when Belle explained the android's part in capturing the infamous dog-fighting ringleader. She congratulated everyone on their heroism and thanked them for their help in stopping Punkin's criminal activities.

As the two families left the authorities' building, they were greeted by a bright and sunny day.

"Today's our last day in Tharsis. Let's do something just for fun," Yun said. "We have much to celebrate."

"And I've had enough adventure to last a lifetime," Belle laughed.

"As have I," added Ta'al.

They spent the rest of the morning at the Nabian natural history museum. Belle and Ta'al enjoyed learning about all sorts of creatures from the Nabian home world.

During lunch, Zara and Yun received a final message from the doctor at the hospital.

"All is well with me and the baby," Zara announced. "I just needed to adapt to the different gravity on Mars."

Belle heaved a huge sigh of relief. Her mum would be back to her old self soon.

The two families celebrated the rest of the day by doing some shopping. Yun and Zara bought a lovely cot for the new baby. And they bought Belle a real book, made of old Earth paper and ink. Belle couldn't stop smelling it and running her hands over the smooth pages.

Ta'al's parents got her a delicate ceremonial scarf. It changed colour and went from purple to green to orange, depending on how it reflected the sunlight.

On their way back to the hotel, they passed the jewellery shop that Belle had seen the other day. She whispered something to Ta'al, and then told her parents that they'd catch up with them in a minute because something was stuck in her boot.

"Meet us at the cafe across the street," Zara said. "And don't be long."

"We won't," she said. As soon as their parents were out of sight, the girls ducked into the jewellery shop.

"May I help you?" the Parsiv shopkeeper asked. She stared at them with her three eyes.

"I have a bit of money," Belle said. "I'd like to get one of those stones that change colour with the wand."

"Ah, you must mean the moonstones." She went to the counter and placed a tray of jewellery in front of the girls.

"They arrre lovely, but verrry inexpensive," she said. "They arrre common on Parrrsiv. I just rrreceived a large shipment of them. I'm hoping they will become popularrr herrre."

After learning how much Belle could afford, the shopkeeper picked out a simple necklace with moonstones placed in a heart shape.

"It's perfect! That's the one I'll take," she said, holding the delicate necklace against her skin.

The shopkeeper wrapped it in colourful paper and placed it in a box.

"You'll look beautiful with this on," Ta'al said.

"Oh no," Belle replied. "This is for my mum."

Ta'al slipped her arms around Belle and gave her a squeeze. Then, arms locked together, the girls raced across the street to rejoin their families.

"You know," Belle said, "I love being on holiday, but I can't wait to get home."

"Oh, I agree," Ta'al said, smiling. "Give me the quiet of farm life anytime."

Sol 17/Spring, Mars Cycle 106

Our holiday is over, and honestly, I can't say I'm sorry to be leaving. Tharsis City is amazing. But it's too much for me, I think. Funny, isn't it? Only a few months ago, I wanted to go back to Earth and the same kind of city life found in Tharsis.

But I think I've had enough adventures for now. I agree with Ta'al — the quiet farm life is just what I long for. As long as I have Raider snuggled at my feet, and Melody and Ta'al near by, I'll be happy to get back to our boring turkens and shoats, and even school!

ABOUT THE AUTHOR

A.L. Collins learned a lot about writing from her teachers at Hamline University in Minnesota, USA. She has always loved reading science-fiction stories about other worlds and strange aliens. She enjoys creating and writing about new worlds, as well as envisioning what the future might look like. Since writing the Redworld series, she has collected a map of Mars that hangs in her living room and a rotating model of the red planet, which sits on her desk. When not writing, Collins enjoys spending her spare time reading and playing board games with her family. She lives near Seattle, Washington, USA, with her husband and five dogs.

• • • • **•** • • •

ABOUT THE ILLUSTRATOR

Tomislav Tikulin was born in Zagreb, Croatia. Tikulin has extensive experience creating digital artwork for book covers, posters, DVD jackets and production illustrations. Tomislav especially enjoys illustrating tales of science fiction, fantasy and scary stories. His work has also appeared in magazines such as *Fantasy & Science Fiction*, *Asimov's Science Fiction*, *Orson Scott Card's Intergalactic Medicine Show* and *Analog Science Fiction & Fact*. Tomislav is also proud to say that his artwork has graced the covers of many books including Larry Niven's *The Ringworld Engineers*, Arthur C. Clarke's *Rendezvous With Rama* and Ray Bradbury's *Dandelion Wine* (50th anniversary edition).

:WHAT DO YOU THINK?:

1. Think about the incredible things Belle saw in Tharsis City. Have you ever visited a new city with amazing sights? Compare your experiences with Belle's. In what ways was your city adventure similar to or different from hers?

2. Belle and Ta'al used a special computer program as a guide to help them find the mining camp. Can you think of any other ways they could have found the camp where Raider was being kept?

3. Several people are disrespectful to Ta'al and her parents while they wait to visit the desalination plant. Put yourself in Belle's place. How would you react if your friends were treated unfairly because of the way they look?

4. Think about the advertisements Belle's family saw in Tharsis City. Describe three advertisements for amazing sights you might see if you visited Tharsis.

5. Pretend that you are Melody. Think about what it was like for her to be taken away by the SPA people. Write a short story about the experience from her perspective.

:GLOSSARY:

brochure booklet that gives information about a location, product or service

desalination process of removing salt from ocean water

distinctive being different or unique from all others

diverse varied or assorted

expedition journey with a goal, such as exploring or searching for something

ignorant not educated, or not knowing many things

perimeter outer edge or boundary of an area

pregnancy being pregnant; when a woman is expecting to have a baby

terraform change the environment of a planet or moon to make it capable of supporting life